Walt Disney
PICTURES PRESENTS

DINOSAUR

A Junior Novel by Scott Sorrentino

Disney
PRESS

New York

Printed in the United States of America.

First Edition

1 3 5 7 9 10 8 6 4 2

The text for this book is set in 12-point ITC Leawood.

Library of Congress Catalog Card Number: 99-69491

ISBN 0-7868-4407-8

For more Disney Press fun, visit www.disneybooks.com

Prologue

There were twelve eggs in the nest. Twelve eggs that soon would hatch into twelve beautiful dinosaur children. And before you could say "iguanodon," they would be fifteen feet tall and weigh four and a half tons.

A flock of ichthyornis flew gracefully overhead, water cascaded down a nearby waterfall, and the surrounding mountains were almost overbearing in their protective majesty. It was known as the Nesting Grounds, a valley of birth and growth where dinosaurs knew their eggs would be safe.

The mother iguanodon noticed a young parasaurolophus taking an interest in her handiwork. She brushed him away gently with a free foot, but he soon returned. She turned suddenly, scaring him away with an exaggerated snort.

The little parasaurolophus was on a child's mission. He hardly seemed to notice the other mother dinosaurs and their nests as he made his way through the thick foliage. In the clearing ahead, he could see several large brachiosaurs drinking from a sparkling lake. Then he watched as a winged lizard flew into a hollow log and came out the other side with a sticklike insect bulging from the corner of its mouth.

A drop splashed innocently onto a branch in front of the young dinosaur. He looked at it, then sniffed it curiously. It was too thick and gooey to be rain. He watched the strange, syrupy liquid stretch until it dripped onto the ground below. There was a rustle of trees, and he heard a low, menacing growl. He looked around, suddenly fearful, but all the little parasaurolophus could see were flashes of white through the brush—*TEETH!* Teeth oozing with thick, gooey saliva. It was a carnotaur! He turned and fled.

The powerful carnotaur uprooted trees and destroyed everything in its path as it chased the young parasaurolophus, who was running as fast as his little legs could carry him. The giant beast blazed through the forest with terrifying speed, and was about to overtake the smaller dinosaur, but then suddenly surged right past him.

A parasaurolophus was just an appetizer, and the carnotaur wasn't interested in an appetizer. He was looking for a real meal.

The herd of dinosaurs in the Nesting Grounds were caught unaware as the carnotaur burst through the trees. Within seconds, the peaceful tranquility of the valley turned to chaos and panic. The Herd scattered, stampeding away from the raging beast.

Moments later, with a deafening wail, the carnotaur smashed the nest full of eggs. Looking around, he finally spotted his first course—a slow-footed styracosaur. Without warning, the carnotaur pounced on the helpless animal, roaring triumphantly.

As the terrifying roar echoed through the

valley, a soft breeze blew gently through the trees surrounding the iguanodon nest. Eleven of the eggs were destroyed, but one had miraculously survived.

In the aftermath of destruction, an oviraptor snatched the egg from the nest and brought it to a jagged rock where he tried to crack it open. He caught the attention of one of his mates, and soon they were recklessly fighting over the egg. With all the clawing and pulling, the egg popped free, plunging over the cliff into a river hundreds of feet below.

A labyrinthodont caught sight of the large egg sinking through the rushing water. He swallowed the egg, but quickly spit it out. Yuck!

The egg continued along with the current, bobbing its way downstream. A giant pteranodon spotted it from the air and swooped down and snatched the egg from the water. Without delay, the pteranodon made its way home to a nearby island.

A flock of ichthyornis spotted the egg from the ground, and flew at the pteranodon, trying to steal the egg midair. Fighting off the nasty birds, the pteranodon lost its grip on the egg and it slipped away, disappearing through the clouds.

The calm serenity of Lemur Island was suddenly broken as the egg crashed through the thick, leafy branches of the towering trees, plunging toward the forest floor. It finally landed in the outstretched branches of a huge tree, cradled delicately.

It was round and spotted, and no tree-dwelling, vine-swinging, run-of-the-forest lemur had ever seen anything like it before. A few lemurs slowly approached.

"Yar, what is it?" little Zini asked. They were looking at this thing that had just fallen from the sky. To their amazement, it had landed safely, high in the outstretched branches of a large tree.

"I don't know," Yar grunted.

Plio climbed up ahead, determined to get a better look.

"Plio! Get back here," Yar whispered loudly. "We don't know what it is!"

She wasn't listening. With cautious steps, she moved toward the object. It was big, and something seemed to be moving inside.

With a loud *CRACK*, it started to open and Plio drew back, startled.

"Dad . . . get over here," she called.

Yar approached carefully. "Well, what is it?" he asked.

"It *was* an egg," Plio said, still facing away from them. Then she turned slowly, revealing a creature cradled in her arms the likes of which had never been seen on Lemur Island.

It was a baby dinosaur.

Yar shrieked. "It's a coldblooded monster from across the sea. Vicious, flesh eating . . ."

"Looks like a baby to me," Plio said. She couldn't help feeling a kind of motherly love for the new arrival. Sure, it was a dinosaur, but it was also a baby.

"Babies grow up!" Yar insisted. "You keep that thing, one day we'll turn our backs, and it'll be picking us out of its teeth!"

"What's gotten into you, Dad?" asked Plio.

"Plio, that thing is dangerous."

Plio looked into its happy, wide eyes. It was too cute to be dangerous.

"I'm sorry, little one," she told it gently.

Then she held it out to Yar, who took it into his arms awkwardly. "Okay, get rid of it," she added casually.

Yar was caught off guard.

"Huh?" he said, almost dropping the dinosaur. Plio grunted, turning her back.

Yar composed himself. "All right," he announced, "I will."

The group of lemurs watched as Yar stepped to the edge of the branch, holding the little dino out to be dropped into the dark forest below. It was a long way down.

"You better hurry up, Dad," Plio teased. "It looks hungry."

Yar grumbled to himself. Suddenly he could feel everyone staring at him. Even the little dinosaur opened its eyes and looked at him curiously.

That was it. He couldn't do it.

"Here . . ." Yar said to Plio, handing the baby back to her and turning to walk away.

"It's okay, Dad," Plio called after him. "We'll teach it to hate meat."

Zini hopped closer, finally getting a good look at the baby.

"This monster's got no teeth," he noticed. "What's he gonna do, gum us to death?"

"Zini, come on," Plio smiled. "Look at that sweet little face. Does that look like a monster to you?"

Chapter 1

"**A**RRRRRRRRRR!" the monster roared, causing the lemurs to scatter in terror.

The earth shook as the monster's giant feet stomped through the forest, crushing trees and snapping branches with every step. The lemurs scurried ahead onto a fallen tree that had created a convenient bridge across a deep gorge. But one of the lemurs had fallen behind. It was Suri, Plio's daughter. With the monster close behind, she scampered up a tree, trying to get away. But the tree was no problem for the monster. He was a full-grown iguanodon, and he could easily reach Suri with his outstretched neck.

In desperation, Suri leaped from the

branch, but the monster caught her midair, swallowing her whole—except for her tail, which was still sticking out of his mouth, wagging back and forth. The monster's eyes widened as he casually slurped in the tail like a wet noodle.

Then the monster snarled at the lemurs on the ground, who cowered in fear.

Suddenly, they heard muffled cries coming from inside his mouth.

"Let me out!" Suri was saying. "Let me out!"

The monster's eyes widened as he swirled Suri around in his mouth. Then . . . PTOOOEY! He spit her onto the ground.

"Bleccchhh . . . hairball!" he complained.

Suri stood up, drenched in dino-slobber. "That was grrrreat!"

Of course, the monster wasn't really a monster at all. He was the baby "monster" that had grown up. His name was Aladar, and since he was the only dinosaur on Lemur Island, they loved to play this game.

"GET HIM!" Suri cried, leaping onto Aladar's back.

The rest of the lemurs joined in the fun, tickling Aladar and clinging to his legs and tail.

"Oh, no!" he giggled., "Attacking lemurs!"

There was a lot of tickling going on, and Aladar was laughing so hard it was starting to hurt.

"Okay, you got me, you got me! Uncle! No, stop! STOP!"

Suddenly Aladar collapsed, slumping down against a fallen tree with his tongue hanging out.

The little lemurs stared in disbelief.

Suri went over for a closer look. "Aladar. . . ?" she said. "You're not dead . . . are you?"

Aladar grinned, his eyes opening wide. They shrieked happily, bouncing up and down on Aladar's soft stomach like it was a trampoline.

"All right, guys, break it up," came a voice from out of the nearby trees.

It was Plio—older, wiser, and still beautiful. "Remember the courtship ceremony," she added. "You're gonna miss all that smooching."

"Awww, Mom," Suri protested.

"That's okay, Plio," said Aladar. "We can smooch right here."

He leaned forward, ready to cover them with his infamous dino-slobber. They giggled and scampered back into the forest.

Suri was also giggling as she climbed aboard her mom's back for the ride home.

"It's a shame you don't like kids," Plio said to Aladar.

"Eew!" he joked. "Nasty little vermin."

"Why don't you go find Zini," she said, heading away. "He's rehearsing pick-up lines. Let's hope he has some new material."

Aladar found Zini at the beach. He was now a teenager. As Aladar watched from the edge of the forest, his best friend paced nervously back and forth.

"Hey, sweetie," he said to his invisible partner, "if you'll be my bride, I'll groom ya."

He stopped pacing, thinking this through. "That's good. . . . Oh, that's good." Taking a deep breath, he continued. "Girls, I am known as the professor of love—and school is *in session*." He was even happier with that one. "Yeah, I still got it!"

"I hope it's not contagious," Aladar said, joining Zini by the water's edge. Zini looked up, embarrassed. "C'mon, hot stuff," Aladar continued. "Let's get going. You don't want to miss Yar's annual pep talk."

"Oh, goody . . . I can't wait to hear the mating advice of an old monkey."

"Hey, hey, hey," Aladar said as they began to walk back toward the forest. "I heard that in his day, that old monkey was quite a swinger."

"You talkin' about Yar?"

"Yeah! To hear him tell it, he put the prime in primate."

"Really . . ." Zini said, not convinced.

They headed toward the Ritual Tree, which stood firm and steady against the warm afternoon sky.

Chapter

2

In the heart of the forest, Yar presided over the group of young male lemurs. It was time to impart some of his vast knowledge regarding the opposite sex, and to prepare them for the courtship ritual. It was time to teach lemurs the art of *l'amour*.

"Okay, boys," he began, "Listen and learn from the master . . ."

At the same time, not far away, Plio and the girls gathered under the Ritual Tree for their own assembly.

"Now, girls," she said. "Don't jump into the trees after the first boy with a cute back flip." The girls began to giggle. "It's more fun if you keep them guessing . . ."

"And if a cute back flip doesn't work . . ." Yar instructed, "guess!" The boys nodded in agreement.

Plio told the girls: "You're never going to forget this day, so make it one to remember."

While Yar added to the boys: "But . . . if you mess up, don't worry. They'll never remember."

That was Aladar's cue. He made his entrance dramatically, ready to ferry the boys away to pair up with the most terrifying creatures on Lemur Island—girls.

"C'mon, guys," he said, "we don't want to let 'em down."

Yar stood up and addressed the troops with some final words of wisdom. "Chest out! Chin up!" he commanded. "Make 'em look good!" he called as Aladar lumbered away with his load.

Aladar paraded up to the Ritual Tree, showing off his manly cargo.

"Hey, girls, look who just pulled into town! Your buffet table of love!" he shouted.

The girls laughed nervously as the boys

started to show off. Zini was one of the first to make a pass. "Hey, free samples," he shouted. "Get me while I'm hot." He twirled himself into a frenzy, almost falling off Aladar's back.

At a safe distance, Yar and Plio observed the proceedings with amusement.

The boys began to leap into the trees, swinging, flipping, hooting, and hollering. The girls, taking their cue from Plio, pretended not to be interested. These boys were going to have to work hard to impress them.

Zini continued to struggle. He leaped into the air, completely missing the vine he had hoped to grab gracefully with one hand while waving to the girls with the other. Instead, he tumbled into a bush and found himself stuck in the crook of a branch.

"Oh, boy," he muttered, trying to break free.

Fortunately, Aladar was there to help.

"You're missing all the action, pal!"

"Hey, haven't you heard?" Zini said. "I am the action!"

Aladar grabbed the branch between his

teeth and sling-shot Zini toward the Ritual Tree. Flying through the air, Zini managed a quick wink at the girls as he grabbed a vine and swung out of control. Aladar shook his head.

As the other boys continued to show off, the girls could no longer pretend to ignore them. With flowers in their mouths, they joined the party, leaping from vine to vine alongside the boys, flirting, teasing, and searching for "the one." One by one, as was the custom, the girls offered a flower to their chosen partner. The flirting had ended, and courtship had begun.

And once again, as was becoming a custom, Zini found himself cut off from the group, caught in a tangle of vines. He could only helplessly watch as the others paired off and retreated happily into the forest.

Aladar watched with a strange combination of joy and longing. On one hand, he was glad for the happy couples. But he also felt alone. There were no dinosaur mates for him, and he would never be a part of the courtship ritual.

Then he noticed Zini, who had finally freed himself from the knotted vines.

"Don't worry," Aladar said hopefully, "you always have next year."

Zini attempted a smile, but there was just no hiding his disappointment. He made his way off into the deep forest to be alone.

As Aladar watched his friend disappear into the trees, Plio joined him.

"Well," she said, "it's never really been his best event."

"He's got a tougher hide than mine," Aladar said.

"Oh, Aladar," Plio comforted, "if only there was someone on the island for you, someone who looks like you, but prettier."

Aladar smiled. "Aww, c'mon, Plio," he said. "What more could I want?"

And for a moment, they just stared out past the Ritual Tree toward the vast ocean, enjoying the simple beauty that surrounded them.

Chapter

3

The serenity was soon interrupted by the unmistakable presence of danger. Not far away, Yar was busy congratulating himself on a job well done, when he sniffed something strange. He sniffed again.

Suddenly there was a streak of bright light. Then another. And another. A shower of sparkling light trailed across the sky.

"What are they?" asked Suri, scampering over to Aladar.

"I don't know," Aladar replied.

The other lemurs began to gather on the cliff, looking up into the sky. Suri leaped up onto a branch of the Ritual Tree to get a better look. A stiff breeze rustled the branches around her. Then there were a series of flashes, longer this time. The brilliant, glittery light rippled across the sky.

A flock of birds suddenly took flight, frantically flapping into the sky. As the fireworks continued, the terrified birds dodged the streaking lights, scattering out over the open sea.

"Dad . . ." Plio whispered, moving closer to Yar.

"Something's wrong," Yar said softly.

Plio looked around for Suri. "Aladar, where's Suri?"

"She's up in the . . . tree. . . ."

Aladar trailed off as a giant fireball emerged from the fireworks. Lit with a terrifying glow, the Fireball screamed by overhead and disappeared over the horizon. Suddenly it was intensely quiet . . . and dark.

The lemurs huddled together, wondering what they had just seen. Moments later they began to hear a strange, shrill sound. It grew louder as the ground quaked slightly.

Suddenly, a shockwave hit full force, knocking them all backward, tumbling end over end.

"C'mon! Go! Go!" Plio shouted to the others, hoping to organize some kind of retreat.

"Mom!" Suri cried from a branch high in the tree.

"Suri!" Aladar called out.

"Mom!" she cried again.

Plio was already on her way. She climbed up the tree and grabbed Suri as flaming debris exploded everywhere.

The terrified lemurs were fleeing in every direction as more and more fireballs exploded around them. Aladar stopped under the Ritual Tree just long enough for Plio and Suri to leap onto his back.

"Run, Aladar!" Plio cried as the big dinosaur took off. Yar was just ahead, waving frantically.

"Yar, c'mon!" Aladar shouted.

Aladar nudged Yar onto his back. He was about to surge ahead when a burning tree collapsed in front of him, blocking the way. Turning quickly, he lurched forward and accelerated to full speed. Burning rocks continued to rain down on Lemur Island like a fiery blizzard.

Up ahead, Aladar caught sight of Zini.

"Zini, jump!!" Aladar yelled to him.

Plio reached out and pulled Zini onto Aladar just as a flaming rock crashed into the spot where he had just been running.

"Hold on!" Plio commanded. Behind them they could see a giant wave of fire headed toward the island. It was growing larger, swallowing the sky as it made its deadly approach. When it hit land, it pulverized the Ritual Tree like a nuclear blast. The fire blanketed the forest, burning everything in its path. Aladar and the others could feel the heat at their backs as they broke through the forest.

At the edge of a sheer cliff, Aladar screeched to a halt. It was a long way down, but there was no time to think. The fire was going to overtake them soon.

He leaped off the cliff just as the wall of fire blazed over their heads. The terrified dinosaur and his lemur family plunged down the steep cliff into the foaming water below. Overhead, a series of eruptions sprayed the remains of Lemur Island all around them.

Aladar was the first to surface, coughing buckets of water and gasping for air.

"PLIO! YAR! WHERE ARE YOU?" he called out, but there was no answer.

"ALADAR!" he heard a voice cry. It was Plio. "Over here!" Aladar turned, and sure enough, there they all were. It was a miracle!

Aladar swam toward them as fast as he could, waves crashing down around him. Navigating his way through the burning debris, he was soon reunited with his family. They huddled close together in the water, for the moment just happy to be alive.

With Zini, Plio, Suri, and Yar aboard, Aladar staggered out of the water, exhausted. After a long swim, they had reached the mainland. They only hoped that others had made it as well.

The beach had been hit hard. Hot, glowing rocks and the smoldering remains of trees and bark were scattered everywhere. They could barely see through the thick smoke, but looking around, they found no sign of any kind of life.

Aladar stumbled forward and collapsed as the weary lemurs slid off him, coughing and choking.

Suri began to look around for any sign of the others, but it was no use. In the distance, she could see the burning island that used to be their home. They were the only ones who had made it safely to the shore.

Overcome with sadness, Suri let out a desperate lemur call that hovered in the still air like an eerie fog. There was no answer. She called out again, an urgent plea for some kind of response. Aladar came up beside her and bellowed his own version of the call. Silence. Suri began to cry.

Plio pulled her into her arms. "Oh, Suri," she said softly. "Easy . . . easy."

"It's gone," Suri said, her voice quivering. "They're all gone."

Yar and Zini joined them. They wanted to be hopeful, but it was hard. Everything they had ever known was suddenly gone. What were they going to do?

"C'mon," Aladar said sadly. "We can't stay here."

One by one, the lemurs climbed aboard the weary dinosaur, and then turned to take a last look at what was left of Lemur Island. That was behind them now. In front of them was the dark, desolate future. Aladar summoned all his remaining strength and lumbered forward.

Chapter

4

It was a long, difficult night, and Aladar's endurance was being tested. The group had made their way onto a wide plateau. They were hot and thirsty, and the dry, scorching wind wasn't helping things. It was so different from the cool, moist morning air on Lemur Island. Signs of the previous day's disaster were every-where, and the morning sunlight showed the full extent of the destruction. But the group marched onward, searching, hoping . . .

Shortly after dawn, Aladar spotted a brown pool of water. But as soon as he tasted it, he spit it out. Once again, a glimmer of hope was dashed and they pressed onward.

Suri whimpered softly, holding a hand in

front of her eyes to protect herself from the harsh wind and flying dust.

"Now, now, Suri," Yar comforted her. "There's nothing to be afraid of."

Zini suddenly tapped Yar hard on the shoulder.

"Look!" cried Zini, pointing ahead.

Aladar stopped in his tracks. There was some kind of animal disappearing over the ridge.

"Did ya see that?" asked Aladar. He blinked rapidly to make sure his eyes were working.

"See what?" answered Yar.

"I did," Zini declared.

"Me, too," Suri confirmed.

So Aladar wasn't seeing things. He decided to get a closer look. With lemurs in tow, he rushed up to the ridge where the animal had disappeared. There was a gully below, but no sign of any animal.

"Where did it go?" asked Plio.

"I don't know," Aladar replied, even more determined now. "Let's go see."

"Leave it alone," Yar said. "It's scaring Suri."

"No, it's not," Suri protested.

"Everyone just be quiet." Aladar moved cautiously into the gully. He looked around, his eyes wide and hopeful, but there was no sign of the creature. Only the hot wind whistling through the canyons. Then he heard something . . .

CLICK, CLICK, CLICK . . .

Aladar and the others looked in the direction of the clicking sound. Up ahead on the ridge, a beautiful, multicolored dinosaur was staring down at them. At least they thought it was a dinosaur. It didn't look exactly like Aladar, but it definitely wasn't a lemur.

CLICK, CLICK, CLICK . . .

Now there was another one of the colorful creatures . . . then another, and another. They seemed to be everywhere. Were there other survivors?

"*Ssssss!*" The creature bared its teeth viciously. These definitely weren't friendly dinosaurs. They were raptors!

Aladar jumped back as the lemurs, caught off guard, momentarily lost their balance.

The raptors seized the opportunity. They

ran at Aladar in turns, nipping at him from all directions before rushing away again. It was a test of his defenses.

Aladar kicked one away and turned to face another, but more of them moved in, surrounding him.

"*Sssssss!*" Several raptors lunged at Aladar. But Aladar leaped over the raptors and landed safely on a large boulder nearby.

Aladar raced up the other side of the gully to the next ridge and found himself on a plateau. The lemurs continued to cling to him for dear life.

"YEOW!" Aladar yelped as one of the raptors bit down on his leg. He kicked it off and kept running.

Yar suddenly lost his grip and slid over the edge.

"Grab on!" Zini yelled, leaning down as far as he could and reaching out with his free hand.

"I can't reach!" Yar yelled back, barely hanging on.

With Plio's help they were able to pull Yar back up just in time. *SNAP!* A raptor's teeth closed down on the empty space where Yar had just been hanging.

One of the raptors was so close now that Aladar could feel its breath on his body. Just when he thought the raptor was going to attack, it slowed down.

"Aladar," Plio cried triumphantly, "they're stopping!"

Sure enough, the raptors had broken off their pursuit. But before the group could begin their celebration, the ground began to tremble.

The tremor grew rapidly into a rumble. Aladar looked up to see a giant dust cloud heading straight for them!

A monstrous shape suddenly burst through the dust cloud, knocking Aladar to the ground. Aladar looked up into the face of . . . another Aladar! The face was different from Aladar's— harder, with burning eyes and crinkled lips, but it was definitely an iguanodon face.

"OUT OF MY WAY!" roared the massive figure before continuing on its way. Aladar wasn't quite sure what was going on. He struggled to his feet, only to be unceremoniously shoved back by another iguanodon.

"You heard Kron!" the second one roared. "Move it!"

Now more shapes went thundering past. Aladar dodged and weaved as Plio and the others clung to his back. He could barely see through all the dust, and the noise was deafening. Several smaller shapes emerged from the dust and scurried underneath Aladar. They were little dinosaurs, and they were using Aladar for cover.

WHAM!

Aladar's head butted against something— another iguanodon. But this one was different . . . pretty.

"Oww!" she said, surprising him. "Watch it!"

Then with a disgusted snort, she pushed right past him and continued on her way. Aladar was speechless.

If the ground had been shaking before, now it was pounding. A few giant steps away, and headed right toward them, was the largest, most magnificent animal any of them had ever seen before. Each of its legs looked as big as Aladar himself, and all he could do was crouch down as the enormous brachiosaur, the largest creature ever to walk the earth, thundered over him and continued on her way.

"Walking backward, huh?" said a weary voice.

They all turned to see an older styracosaur moving slowly along the same path as the others. "Let me know if that gets you there any faster," she added, waddling past them. "Keep those little legs moving, Url," she called over her shoulder, "or you'll get left behind." Behind her, a small ankylosaur was bringing up the rear—her pet dino.

The dust was finally settling and now the group had a better view of what they had just encountered. Moving down the bluff toward a rocky mesa was an enormous herd of dinosaurs!

"Look at all the Aladars!" Suri exclaimed.

Aladar could hardly believe it. A whole herd of fellow dinosaurs! Here were animals just like him! He was no longer alone.

"If you're even thinking of joining up—" Yar began, then stopped abruptly. He heard a noise.

CLICK, CLICK, CLICK . . . raptors!

"Hang on!" Aladar shouted to the lemurs as he bounded down the slope to find the dinosaur herd. "Hang on!"

The raptors sneered angrily as they watched their dinner get away.

Chapter
5

Kron surveyed the landscape around him. The Herd had been moving all day and was visibly tired. They had reached the foot of a hill, which was surrounded by stony, desolate terrain. Not ideal, but it would do. Bruton, his lieutenant, approached with news.

"Kron, there's a more protected spot farther down—"

"We'll rest here for the night," Kron said, his mind made up. "Send them up."

Bruton nodded and turned to face the Herd, bellowing out the command.

At the back of the Herd, Aladar and the others

heard Bruton's mighty bellow, but they didn't have a clue what it meant. The answer came soon enough as they watched the Herd in a mad scramble to secure sleeping space for the night. There was pushing, shoving—every dinosaur for itself. Aladar and his lemur companions were uncertain where they fit into it all.

"Oh, Eema," a voice moaned, "I wish we were at your Nesting Grounds now."

They turned to see the huge brachiosaur that had almost trampled them looking around nervously. She was the biggest animal they had ever seen, though she seemed as lost and confused as they were.

"All this pushing and shoving about, just for a place to sleep," she said. "I'm not used to this kind of behavior."

"Baylene, you got big feet," another voice said. This one belonged to the older, slower styracosaur that had passed them earlier. "Just give 'em a kick."

"Oh, I couldn't possibly . . ." protested Baylene, as several smaller dinosaurs jockeyed for a place. "Shoo! Shoo!" she said to the little dinos at her feet. They barely noticed. Eema gave a snort and scared them away.

"Come on, Baylene!" Eema said. She was fast losing her patience with her gigantic friend. "Ya wanna get to the Nesting Grounds alive, show some backbone."

Just as they were ready to settle in for the night, Aladar came over to introduce himself.

"Hey, there," Aladar greeted them cheerfully.

Eema was startled and Baylene let out a gasp.

"Sorry about that," he continued awkwardly. "It's just that we overheard you talking . . . and, uh . . ."

Aladar was being distracted by the anky-losaur nudging at his feet. The little tyke had brought over a slobbery rock and apparently wanted to play.

"Well, my word, look at Url," Eema exclaimed to Baylene. "He doesn't normally warm up to strangers so fast."

"My name's Aladar. This is my family. We're all that's left," Aladar said.

"Oh, my dear, I'm so sorry," Baylene said.

"Baylene's the last of her kind. Finding

stragglers like her all along the way," Eema added.

"We heard you say something about nesting grounds," Plio said.

"It's the most beautiful place," Eema sighed. "It's where the Herd goes to have their babies. But that Fireball put us back a spell, and the eggs could come 'fore we get there," Eema told them.

"Will we find anybody that looks like us there?" Suri asked hopefully.

"Who knows what we'll find," Eema said. "The hard job now is just getting there."

"And we're being driven unmercifully by Kron," Baylene added, "the head honcho."

"Then tell him to slow down," Aladar suggested. "What's the worst he can do?"

As if on cue, three ominous dinosaur figures emerged from the darkness and marched straight past them, the biggest one shoving Aladar out of the way as he passed.

"Hey!" Aladar shouted after him. There was no response. "What's his problem?" he asked.

"That's him, honey," Eema whispered, "Kron."

Perfect! Just the dino he wanted to see. Aladar headed off after them, calling out as he approached.

"Uh . . . excuse me . . . Kron?"

Aladar was sure that if Kron was made aware of the problems his friends were having . . . "Got a second?" Aladar asked hopefully.

Bruton turned abruptly. "Get lost, kid!" he snapped.

"Relax, Bruton," Kron said, taking charge of the situation. He turned and approached Aladar, giving the iguanodon the once-over. "Who are you?"

The question took Aladar by surprise.

"Uh, Aladar," he managed to say finally.

"Why aren't you uphill with the youngbloods?" Kron asked sternly.

"Well, I was back here talking to these guys," Aladar began. "I guess they're having a hard time keeping up," Aladar explained. "So, you know," he continued, "maybe you could slow it down a bit?"

Kron seemed to consider Aladar's request for a moment.

"Hmm . . ." he mused sarcastically. "Let the *weak* set the pace. Now there's an idea. Better let me do the thinking from now on, Aladar," he advised as he headed off. Aladar was insulted, but he wasn't about to give up.

"Hey, they need help back there," Aladar protested.

Kron turned back and gave him a cold, hard stare. "Watch yourself, boy," he warned. And with that, he marched away, with Bruton close behind.

Neera started off as well, but paused to give Aladar a word of encouragement.

"Don't worry," she whispered. "That's how my brother treats all newcomers." Then she added, smiling, "No matter how charming they are."

Before Aladar could react, she left to rejoin her brother and his friend.

"You sure know how to catch a girl's eye there, stud," Zini crowed.

"I wouldn't be catching nobody's eye, if I was you," Eema warned. She'd been watching and listening from a safe distance, but now she joined them. "'Specially Neera's!"

she continued. "You just keep your head down and mind what Kron tells you."

Neera. Aladar rolled the name around in his head. He was looking forward to getting to know her better, now that they had more or less decided to be a part of the march to the Nesting Grounds. Better to go along with the rest of the Herd than to take their chances with the raptors. But he couldn't worry about that right now. It was bedtime, he was exhausted, and for the first time in his life, he had a beautiful girl to dream about.

Chapter
6

The next morning, Aladar was awakened by someone nudging him. It was Zini, and he was in a panic. Apparently, the Herd was already up and getting ready to move out. Aladar picked himself up as fast as he could and they set off. As they made their way through the Herd, Zini spotted Neera walking along with a couple of young dinos in tow.

"Hey, there's your girlfriend!"

"What are you talking about?" Aladar asked.

"You know . . . Neeeera," he teased. "Scaly skin . . . yellow eyes . . . big ankles . . ."

"Yeah, I made a real impression on her," Aladar said, shaking his head.

"What you need is a little help from *the love monkey*," Zini said. Before Aladar could stop him, he called out to Neera.

"Whoa—baby, baby!"

Zini conveniently ducked behind Aladar's neck just as Neera turned. Aladar could only smile at her weakly.

"That, children," she said to the two young dinos, "is what's known as a jerk-a-saurus." And she and the two dinos moved off to join the rest of the Herd.

Neera's brother, meanwhile, was conferring with Bruton regarding the orders for the day.

"We've got a lot of first-timers here," Kron told Bruton. "Make sure they get it. We stop for nothing . . . and no one." Bruton bellowed to the Herd for attention.

"If this is your first crossing, listen up," he shouted. "There is no water till we reach the other side. And you better keep up. 'Cause if a predator catches you, you're on your own." He paused briefly to let the message sink in. "Move out!"

It was tough going. There was no water.

The sun beat down mercilessly, and there was no shade or shelter of any kind. All they could do was keep plodding on, with only the promise of the lush Nesting Grounds to keep up their spirits.

It was especially hard on Eema and Baylene. Eema, who was quite a bit older, was exhausted. But Kron kept ordering them to pick up the pace. They knew they had to get to the Nesting Grounds, and crossing the desert was the only way.

With Aladar, the lemurs, Eema, Baylene, and Url bringing up the rear, they were soon dubbed "the misfits" by the rest of the Herd because they were such a strange group. As the hours passed, they continued to fall further and further behind. The midday sun was oppressive, and Eema was weary from the heat and the pace. She slowed down at times, but she never stopped.

"Hey, old girl, you're wandering off a bit," Yar said as Eema veered off the path at one point.

"That's all I need. A monkey on my back!" Eema joked.

Later that day, they passed the carcass of a dead dinosaur who had succumbed to the heat. Eema was wheezing hard now. She plodded along a few more steps, took a full lung's worth of hot, desert air, and promptly collapsed.

Aladar rushed to her side.

"On your feet, Eema!" he coaxed. "You can't let those raptors get to you. They're out there waiting." Helped by Aladar, Eema rose to her feet and once again began to trudge slowly forward.

Behind them, unseen by the Herd, the raptors were getting bolder. They knew the Herd was weakening and that it was only a matter of time. The carnotaurs were also in pursuit close behind—closer than the Herd knew.

Chapter
7

Kron stood at the base of the hill, testing the soil with his foot. The lake was just over this rise. He turned to Bruton, satisfied. Together, they trumpeted the news to the Herd, loud enough that even the misfits way at the back could hear.

"The lake!" exclaimed Eema, with as much excitement as her tired old body could muster.

"We made it?" asked Yar, relieved.

"It's just over that hill, baby!" Eema cackled. But despite her enthusiasm, she was having trouble keeping up.

"Come on, Eema!" Aladar encouraged her. "Water! Remember 'water'? The wet stuff?"

"Time to refresh my memory!" she replied, and picked up her pace slightly.

Kron struggled to the top of the dune, then stopped abruptly. Bruton and Neera joined him. The rest of the Herd followed in due course.

"I'm just gonna walk right into that lake until the water's up to my eyeballs and soak it all in," Eema announced as she labored to join the others at the crest of the dune. But when she got there, she collapsed again—this time out of sheer disbelief.

There was no water. No lake. Only a dry lake bed with the bleached bones of a dead dinosaur.

The Herd stood in stunned silence.

"Maybe the rains collected somewhere else," Bruton finally suggested. Kron stared at the empty lake bed, dumbfounded.

Now the rest of the Herd was becoming alarmed.

"What do you want us to do?" Bruton asked.

"Take a scout," Kron ordered. "Check up ahead."

Bruton nodded gravely and hurried off while Kron turned his attention to the Herd. Panic and fear were spreading. He had to take action.

"The Nesting Grounds are only a few days away," he shouted to the Herd. "Keep moving!" The Herd let out a collective groan. Neera rushed up to her brother.

"Kron, we've never gone this long without water. If we keep going like this, we'll lose half the Herd." She didn't like to question her brother, but someone had to say it.

"Then we save the half that deserves to live," her brother replied. He turned away and moved off to another part of the Herd, bellowing even louder.

Neera stood speechless, shocked by Kron's indifference. She knew he was cold-blooded, but he'd never been this ruthless.

Eema did not believe it. She refused to believe it. She even trudged down the hill towards the dry lake bed.

"Always water here before . . ." she muttered to herself, as though by saying it, she could make it so. She lay in the dirt and rolled back and forth, delirious from the heat. The rest of the Herd just ignored her, and began to move out again as Kron had ordered. Aladar noticed Eema had wandered off and rushed to her side.

"We always had water . . . always . . ." Eema babbled. "Nice water and plenty of mud . . ." She rolled in the dust as the rest of the Herd continued ahead.

"Oh, Eema, please," Baylene begged from the edge of the lake bed. "The Herd won't wait. We must carry on."

But there was no reasoning with her. Eema seemed content to stay right where she was, with or without water. Aladar tried to push her up, but Eema would not budge. Even Baylene came forward to help, and that's when . . .

CRACK!

Aladar turned in the direction of the sound.

CRACK! CRACK!

It seemed to be coming from Baylene's direction.

"Baylene, don't move," he instructed.

"What is it?" she asked, full of concern.

"What's wrong?" Her foot came down again with a loud—*CRACK!*

"Do ya hear that?" asked Zini.

"I sure do," Aladar replied, a smile beginning to form on his face. "Baylene, lift your foot."

Baylene did as she was told, and Aladar and Zini rushed over and began digging around the area where her foot had just been.

"Now press down . . ." Aladar requested.

Baylene stepped down, putting all of her weight on one side, and the dry earth gave way. To their amazement, a pool of water circled around her foot.

"Oh, my goodness!" she exclaimed.

"Water!" yelled Aladar. Then he turned to the Herd and shouted even louder: "Water! C'mon!"

Up on the ridge, Neera heard Aladar's call and turned to see what was going on. She watched as the lemurs led Eema to the pool of water that was forming around Baylene. It was starting to make sense now.

"He found water . . ." she murmured, astonished and more than a little impressed.

Kron shoved a couple of orphan dinos aside as he hurriedly made his way back toward Aladar and the others.

"Kron, look!" Aladar explained. "All we had to do was dig and—"

"Good, now get out of the way," Kron interrupted, pushing him aside. He roared at the others who were drinking, scaring them off, and pushed his own face deep into the water.

That was all the Herd needed to see. They stormed forward in a massive surge, ignoring Aladar's pleas for order.

"Wait . . . WAIT!" Aladar shouted. "There's enough for everyone!" Nobody was listening, however. They mobbed the area, crowding out Baylene, who found herself unable to get close enough for a drink even though she was by far the biggest dinosaur there.

Eema was also caught in the crowd, and she didn't have the strength or the size to fight her way out. Aladar was quick to react, squeezing his way through the mob to give Eema a hand. He used his body to shield her as he guided her safely out of harm's way.

Up on the ridge, Neera observed the whole scene. She watched Aladar protect Eema from the pushing, shoving crowd. He was so different from her brother. . . .

Chapter

8

At twilight, Aladar was keeping watch over his group while they rested from the difficult day. Suddenly, a quiet voice caught his attention.

"Don't be afraid. . . . Come on. No one's gonna hurt you." It was Suri. But who was she talking to?

Aladar followed the sound of her voice to the opening of a cave, where Suri was trying to coax out two dinosaur kids.

"The little Aladars haven't had anything to drink," Suri explained. "I think they're scared of me."

Lemurs were strange to them—and scary. Aladar, on the other hand, was one of their kind. He easily convinced them to come out of the cave, and they followed him over to the lake bed, where he showed them how to find water.

"Here," he demonstrated, digging into the dirt. "You just take a foot and press . . ." A pool of water formed around his foot. The two kids pushed forward, shoving Aladar and each other.

"Hey, come on," he scolded. "Knock it off. Let's work together . . . a little teamwork."

And with all three dinos pressing together, they made a much larger pool of water, to the delight of the little dinosaurs.

"So, where are your parents, anyway?" Aladar asked as the little ones slurped up the water.

"A lot of us are on our own now," a voice answered.

Aladar looked up to see Neera coming toward him.

"You like kids, I see," she said, trying to sound casual.

"Well, the skinny ones can be a little chewy," he replied, grinning.

Neera laughed as Aladar took the opportunity to move closer to where she was standing.

"I'm Aladar. The . . . jerk-a-saurus."

"Sorry about that," she said, a little embarrassed.

"You're probably right," Aladar laughed.

"Why did you help that old one?" Neera asked seriously.

"What else could we do?" he asked simply. "Leave her behind?"

"Well, that happens all the time," she replied. "You don't survive if you're not—"

"Strong enough?" Aladar interrupted, finishing her thought.

"Well, yeah."

"Is that you talking? Or your brother?"

She paused, confused. "I don't know . . ."

"Look, Neera. Everyone counts . . . strong, weak . . . doesn't matter." He had to make her understand. "If we all look out for each other, we all stand a better chance of getting to your Nesting Grounds."

"You sound so sure."

"I'm not. But it's all I know. So . . . um . . .

water! I bet you want some water." He started digging.

Neera watched him, not sure what to believe. Her life had been structured a certain way. She looked up to her brother, Kron. She respected him. But there was something about this Aladar.

"Can I try?" she asked.

"Sure. Just press."

She pressed her foot down, producing a small pool of water. Delighted with her success, she moved to make another pool, but this time as she pressed down, her foot slipped and slid right into Aladar's. With their gazes fixed, the two iguanodons slowly bent down to drink at the same time—and bumped heads.

"Oooops . . ." chuckled Aladar.

"Sorry," Neera apologized.

"No, you . . . you first," he insisted.

A slight distance away, three sets of lemur eyes watched the dinosaur version of the courtship ritual. Zini, Plio, and Yar smiled happily, content that their adopted dinosaur had found someone of his own kind.

High up on the hill, still another pair of eyes were taking in the love scene below. Only these eyes—Kron's eyes—disapproved. He was suddenly distracted by the sound of the raptors in the distance. They were getting bolder as they grew more hungry. And . . . something else. He sniffed the air. What was that?

"Kron . . . carnotaurs!" Bruton shouted as he returned from scouting the area. Badly wounded, he hobbled over to Kron.

"What?!" Kron was instantly on his feet. "They've never come this far north."

"The Fireball must have driven them out." A bloodcurdling roar sounded nearby.

"You led them right to us!" Kron accused. "Maybe you can feed them with your hide!"

Bruton dropped his head and took a deep breath. He bellowed loudly to the Herd to move on.

"What's happening?" Aladar asked Neera, noticing the growing commotion.

"My brother's moving the Herd," she explained, though she wasn't sure why they would want to leave so soon.

"Kron!" she shouted as she approached him. "What's going on?"

"Carnotaurs!" he said. "If we don't keep moving, they'll catch up to us."

"But the others in the back will never make it," Aladar said.

"They'll slow down the predators," Kron replied.

"You can't sacrifice them like this!" Aladar cried desperately.

Aladar couldn't believe Kron was serious. He turned to the address the Herd.

"Hold it!" he shouted at them. "That could be you back there . . . " he said to one of them. "Or you!" he yelled at another.

Kron growled viciously and lashed out at Aladar, knocking him down.

"If you ever interfere again," he snarled, towering over Aladar, "I'll kill you!"

Neera rushed to Aladar's side.

"Stay away from him!" Kron ordered his sister.

Neera glared at him. They were locked in a battle of wills, but Kron was not playing games.

Aladar jumped to his feet. Enough was enough. He started toward Kron, but Neera intervened.

"Aladar, no!" she cried. "You just . . . just go! I'll be okay."

Aladar reluctantly turned away and headed back to where the misfits were slowly struggling to their feet.

"Let's go, let's go," he urged them. "Carnotaurs!"

"Carno-whats?" inquired Yar as the lemurs hopped aboard Aladar. He'd never heard of them before.

"Carnotaur," Eema defined. "A mouthful of teeth with a bad attitude."

"Come on, you guys, get on. We're going to get left behind," Aladar shouted urgently as he headed off at a brisk pace. Eema and the other misfits tried to keep up, but it wasn't long before they started falling behind. They were just too old, and it had been such a hard journey already.

"Aladar, slow down!" Plio pleaded.

Aladar looked back. Eema and Baylene were quite a ways behind. Then he looked ahead just in time to see Neera and the two orphan dinos disappearing over a ridge. He wanted to catch up to her—to be with her—but he couldn't leave his friends behind, no matter what. With a heavy sigh, he turned back to join the others.

Back at the lake bed, two carnotaurs were taking a break, drinking from the pool that Aladar had discovered—cocktail hour before dinner. They had made it this far, and they knew it was only a matter of time before they caught up to the Herd.

Chapter
9

Thunder and lightning lit up the night sky as the Herd continued on. A storm was approaching, which wasn't going to make things any easier.

"Oh, joy—blisters," Baylene moaned.

"I got blisters on my blisters," Eema added.

"You don't wanna know where I got blisters," Yar complained. Before anyone else could add a wisecrack, they heard a low, suffering growl.

"What was that?" Eema asked.

"It came from up ahead," Baylene observed, nodding toward a rocky slope.

"Okay," Zini said hopefully, "what's the worst thing it could be?"

"A carnotaur?" Suri suggested.

"Okay," Zini continued, "what's the second worst thing it could be?"

"Two carnotaurs!" Baylene cried. "Oh, my goodness . . . oh, my goodness!"

"That's it, I'm gone," Eema said, turning to leave.

Aladar finally stepped in. "We don't know for sure." He tried to sound positive and upbeat. "It could be the Herd. Let's check it out."

Baylene continued to fret as the group moved cautiously up the hill. Eema was the first to spot the source of the moaning. It was Bruton! Apparently the misfits weren't the only ones left behind.

"What happened?" Aladar asked.

Bruton silently turned away, wincing a little from his wounds. As he turned, Eema noticed a large gash in his thigh.

"Carnotaurs!" she gasped. "We should keep moving."

"We can't just leave him here," Plio said.

"We can if we move fast enough," Eema replied.

Aladar decided to give Bruton another chance. "Hey, uh, you don't look so good," he began. "Let me help you."

"Save your pity," Bruton grumbled. "I just need some rest. Now get away from me."

"Suit yourself," Aladar said.

A lightning flash cracked through the night air, lighting up the whole area for a moment. It was just long enough for Aladar to notice a nearby cave.

"If you change your mind," Aladar added, "We'll be in those caves."

Bruton remained silent, watching as the group made its way into the caves.

"It's dark," Aladar noted as they took refuge in the cave, "but at least it's dry."

"I like dry," Eema said. "It's the dark part I'm having trouble with."

Just then, a bolt of lightning revealed a large shadow.

"It appears we have a visitor," Baylene announced.

It was Bruton, just outside the entrance to

"Bleccchhh . . . hairball!" Aladar complains
as he spits Suri out.

Zini practices his smooth moves
before the courtship ritual.

"You always have next year,"
Aladar tells a disappointed Zini.

WHOOSH! The bright ball of light disappears over the horizon.

As he struggles to stay afloat, Aladar looks around desperately for his lemur family.

WHOA! Aladar has never seen so many
dinosaurs in his whole life!

Aladar and the lemurs are easy prey for the raptors.

"On your feet, Eema!" Aladar urges.

SQUISH! Baylene finds water!

The Nesting Grounds!

KABLAM! Kron wants to get rid of Aladar for good.

The carnotaur has found the Herd!

a needs Aladar's support now more than ever.

the cave. He managed one more step before collapsing. Aladar rushed over to help.

"You comin' in or what?" he asked.

"What is it with you?" Bruton managed to say.

"At least I know enough to get in out of the rain. Now come on. On your feet."

Together the two iguanodons struggled back into the cave. Bruton claimed a spot away from the group.

While the group settled in for the night, Plio noticed a spiky plant growing out of a crack in the cave wall. She approached it curiously, sniffing it and touching it. It seemed familiar to her. She broke off a branch and examined it.

Eema breathed a sigh of relief as she lay down for the first time in what seemed like days. "Who booked this trip anyway?" she groaned.

"Aw, you'll be at the Nesting Grounds soon enough," Aladar replied.

"Well, when I get there I'm gonna give Kron a piece of my mind!" she snorted angrily.

Plio approached Bruton with the spiky plant.

"This plant grew on our island," she told him. "It will make you feel better."

She took the bulb of the plant and broke it, and a strange, gooey liquid oozed out. Bruton snorted as she rubbed the balm into his wounds. It hurt at first, but then he started to feel a little better.

"Why is he doing this?" Bruton asked, nodding toward Aladar. "Pushing them on with false hope . . ."

"It's hope that's gotten us this far," Plio replied.

"But why doesn't he let them accept their fate?" He lowered his head. "I've accepted mine."

"And what is your fate?" Plio asked.

"To die here," he said. "It's the way things are."

"Only if you give up, Bruton," she offered hopefully. "It's your *choice*, not your fate."

Bruton grunted and turned away.

There was no convincing him, so Plio shrugged, leaving him alone as she rejoined the others.

Bruton watched as Aladar and the misfits huddled together, trying to stay warm. He reached out and grabbed the strange plant Plio had brought, pulling it closer.

Chapter

10

Inside the cave, everyone was resting peacefully. The storm, however, was getting worse. Aladar was awakened by a loud thunderclap. A flash of lightning spotlighted two shapes at the entrance to the cave—two terrifying carnotaurs.

Aladar was about to move when he felt a nudge.

"Shhhhhh," came a voice, right next to him. It was Bruton. "Carnotaurs."

The carnotaurs poked their heads into the cave, sniffing. Fortunately, it was still pitch black inside, and they couldn't see the dinosaurs.

"What do we do?" Aladar whispered.

"Wake the others," Bruton said.

Aladar took Bruton's advice and ushered the group further into the cave, warning them not to look back. They were scared, but they remained quiet, until . . .

"Eeeeeeee—" Url squealed, panicking when he spotted the carnotaurs.

Aladar quickly covered Url's mouth and they all stood frozen. The carnotaurs stopped.

Aladar motioned for the group to continue as he found a place to crouch down. The group silently made their way further back into the cave. The ceiling was starting to slope down, and Baylene ducked down, but not far enough. She accidentally bumped her head, knocking a rock loose that bounced and rolled to the front of the cave.

One of the carnotaurs sniffed at it. It had a familiar scent. He pushed his head into the cave and looked around, but it was still too dark. He was so close now that Aladar could smell the creature's breath.

A flash of lightning lit up the cave. In that

moment, the carnotaurs saw Aladar clearly, and they charged at him.

"GO! GO!" Aladar yelled to the group, as he tried to get away. "Move it, Eema!"

Aladar was fast, but not quite fast enough. One of the carnotaurs chomped on his tail, dragging him back.

"ALADARRRR!" Plio cried. She knew he was in trouble.

The two carnotaurs had Aladar trapped, but just as they were ready to attack, Bruton rammed them, knocking them aside.

"I'll hold them off," he told Aladar. "Go help the others."

Aladar hesitated, then nodded, racing off to the others.

The carnotaurs lunged at Bruton. They snapped at him viciously, but he held his own.

"Keep moving!" Aladar told the group. He couldn't let Bruton face the carnotaurs alone and raced back to help him.

Breaking free, Bruton noticed a wobbly pillar barely holding up the front of the cave. With a desperate lunge, Bruton pushed past the carnotaurs and crashed into the pillar with full force.

Before Aladar could react, the whole roof of the cave collapsed on top of Bruton and one of the carnotaurs. The other carnotaur managed to escape the avalanche. The showering rocks were too much for Aladar, who could only watch helplessly.

"Bruton!" Aladar cried as huge chunks of the cave continued to crash down on the creatures until there was no sign of them at all. When the last of the rocks had fallen and the dust had settled, Aladar ran over, clawing at the debris. Bruton was somewhere underneath, and Aladar was determined to find him.

"Bruton!" he coughed through a cloud of dust. He dug deeper, faster. He was getting close to the bottom. He finally uncovered Bruton, but it was too late.

Aladar lowered his head. Plio joined him.

"You did what you could," she said softly.

Some rocks nearby jiggled for a moment. Aladar and Plio rushed back to the others, eager to get as far away as possible before any more carnotaurs came along.

The surviving carnotaur exploded out of the pile. It stopped and glared viciously into the darkness where the group had just fled, then stomped out of the cave.

Chapter
11

Meanwhile, the Herd continued its desperate trek deep into the desolate valley. They were weary to the point of collapse, but Kron insisted they keep moving. A few had already been lost to heat exhaustion. Kron looked back at the pathetic Herd and snorted. The strong would survive. That was the way of things.

Toward the back, the two orphans were having trouble keeping up. One of them finally collapsed, unable to continue. The other stopped, frantic, but no one else would help. Instead, each dinosaur kept moving forward, not caring.

The orphan tugged at his friend, trying to

bring him back to his feet, but it was no use. Then he heard a voice:

"It's okay, we're going to make it." It was Neera, and she was looking down at them, smiling.

"C'mon," she said, helping them to their feet. As they started on their way, Neera couldn't help looking back, but there was no sign of Aladar or the misfits, for as far as the eye could see. She turned sadly, and walked on with the children.

As Aladar and his group continued deeper and deeper into the cave, the darkness was overwhelming. Aladar could barely see his own feet, let alone what lay ahead.

Yar and Zini passed the time by playing a game.

"Okay, let's do it again," Zini said. "I spy with my little eye . . ."

"A rock?" Yar guessed. It was a pretty safe guess considering that there wasn't much else in the cave.

"You got it again," Zini said, impressed. "Oh, you are good."

"I'll tell you what I spy," Eema said, looking at the wall of rocks blocking the way. "A dead end."

They all stared at the boulders. They looked too big to move, even by dinosaur standards.

"What do we do now?" Yar asked.

"I guess we just go back," Aladar said.

Zini began sniffing. "Hold on a second." There was something in the air, though he couldn't quite place it.

"Zini, what is it?" Suri asked.

"Do you smell that?"

Suri sniffed, Yar sniffed—soon they were all sniffing. Zini bounded ahead, following the scent. As the others followed, Zini leaped onto a ledge and started digging at the rocks. Soon a shaft of light appeared through one of the cracks.

"Get a load of that!" Eema shouted.

"Good show," Baylene added.

Aladar knew what had to be done. "Everybody, stand back," he ordered, readying himself for a charge. "We're outta here!"

And with that, he surged forward, ramming against the wall and pushing with all his might. But the wall wouldn't budge. He pushed again, harder this time, and some of the rocks began to shift. Suddenly, the wall collapsed, which blocked their way even further, including the small opening that had given them such hope.

"Noooo!" Aladar cried out. He smashed himself into the rocks, pounding at them. Years of believing that everything happens for the best, that nothing is impossible, that if you work hard enough you can accomplish anything—all of that had just collapsed in his mind like the wall in front of him. He slumped down against the rocks in defeat.

"Aladar," Plio said finally, "we'll go back."

"We're not meant to survive," Aladar said hopelessly.

No one could believe it. Was this Aladar talking? Positive, upbeat Aladar. He was their inspiration. If it wasn't for him, they would all be looking at the inside of a carnotaur's stomach.

Baylene stepped up to say what needed to be said.

"Oh, yes we *were* meant to survive!" she announced.

Aladar turned around, surprised.

"We're here, aren't we?" Baylene continued. "And how dare you waste that good fortune by simply giving up! Shame, shame, shame on you!" She was on a roll now.

"The worst of it is, you allowed an old fool like me to believe I was needed. That I still had a purpose. And do you know what? You were right. And I'm going to go on believing it. I, for one, am not waiting to die here."

With a nod, Baylene marched toward the wall and began to push with all her might. The others joined her in turn, and soon the entire group was pushing against the wall. It still wouldn't budge.

Aladar watched silently. They were trying so hard, and it was all his fault. He lowered his head. Maybe Kron was right. The strong would survive, and they obviously weren't strong enough. He looked up. They were so determined that he couldn't resist feeling a little inspired. His friends needed his help, and he was letting them down. His moment of doubt had passed. Now it was time to act.

Aladar got up and hurried over to the group, joining in the push against the wall. Cracking slightly, then a little more, the wall slowly gave way. The group doubled its effort, hitting the wall again with all the force they could muster.

There was a thunderous rumble as the rest of the rock wall came tumbling down. Aladar, Baylene, Eema, and the lemurs cheered as they watched the rocks rain down in a cloud of dust and stony rubble. Soon the darkness was chased away by bright daylight flooding the cave.

Chapter

12

When the dust had settled, the group moved carefully through the opening they had created. They found themselves standing on the ledge of a mountainside, gazing around in wonder. Stretched out in front of them was a lush valley surrounded by mountains. Just below, a pristine lake shimmered in the warm sunlight. They had reached the Nesting Grounds!

"It's . . . it's untouched," Eema said in disbelief.

For a moment they stood quietly in awe of the breathtaking scene. A flock of birds soared overhead, heading for the lake.

"Our new home," Plio said, smiling.

"And it comes with a pool!" Zini added, laughing. He started down the hillside with Baylene and Suri close behind. Baylene let out an unrestrained trumpet call as she plunged into the lake. After splashing around for a little while, Zini climbed to the top of Baylene's head.

"Cannonball!" he cried as he surfed down the brachiosaur's long neck, leaped off the curve of her back, and cannonballed into the lake.

"Amateur!!" Baylene yelled. She plunged into the water, sending a huge wave Zini's way.

"Look out below," Baylene warned, but Zini was prepared. He caught the swell with perfect timing and the water swept him up gracefully. It was a primitive form of surfing, but fun!

Eema and Aladar remained on the ridge, impressed by the athletic display.

"Not bad," Aladar said. "But I don't get it. Where's the Herd?"

"Not to mention Neera?" Plio teased, joining them.

"Oh, they'll get here," Eema said. "Soon . . . enough. . . ." Her voice trailed off as she turned.

"Eema? What is it?" Aladar asked, sensing something wrong.

"I spoke too soon."

They all looked to see what had caught Eema's eye. The entrance to the canyon on the other side of the lake had collapsed in some kind of landslide. There were huge boulders piled one on top of the other as high as the peaks on either side.

"That's the way we used to get in here," Eema explained.

Nothing was ever going to get through there, and they all knew it. Plus, there was still a carnotaur outside. Aladar suddenly turned away.

"They'll never make it over that!" he declared.

Eema was concerned. "Aladar, wait, wait . . ." she began, aware of what he intended to do. "Kron'll eat you alive."

Aladar had made up his mind. "Let him try," he replied.

Determined to save the Herd, Aladar headed back into the cave. Eema didn't try to stop him. She knew it was no use.

"I just hope Kron's in a listening mood," she said to herself.

Chapter

13

On the other side of the landslide, Kron stared at the rock barrier in disbelief. The way was completely blocked. He couldn't believe it. They were going to have to try to climb over it.

He looked up at the pile of rocks that stretched into the mountains high above. Only the very strongest would be able to make it. Only the very strongest.

Behind him, the Herd stared in stunned silence. What were they going to do? Hopefully Kron had a plan, because they didn't see any way up those rocks, especially as exhausted as they were.

Neera and the orphans pushed their way

through to the front. She told the children to wait for her as she continued ahead to talk to her brother. When she approached, he was deep in thought, considering their options.

"We'll find a way around it," she suggested.

"No," he said, having made up his mind. "We climb it."

At the cave entrance, Aladar knocked the rocks away and found himself exactly where they had been several nights before when the storm had forced them into the cave. He quickly hurried down the hillside, following the path of the Herd.

He had been wandering for some time when he came across the remains of a dead dinosaur. It must have been part of the Herd. One of the weaker ones, as Kron might say. Then Aladar heard something moving nearby, and from the sound of its footsteps, it had to be something huge.

Aladar quickly hid behind a boulder. Whatever it was, it was making a lot of noise. It must be feeding on the dead animal, Aladar thought. And the only thing that would do that was—a carnotaur!

He peered out from behind the boulder. Sure enough, there was the carnotaur. Aladar could only hope it didn't catch his scent. He ran off, intent on finding the Herd.

The carnotaur stopped chewing. It sensed something, and looked in the direction Aladar had just gone.

One at a time, the leaders of the Herd began to climb slowly up the mountain of rocks. But they weren't making much progress.

"Don't give up," Kron shouted at them. "We have to keep trying. Our survival, our future, is over these rocks. Now let's go home!"

It was as inspirational a speech as they were ever going to get from Kron. But even so, some things were just impossible—and climbing over this landslide was one of them.

Then Kron noticed the orphans at Neera's feet. Perfect!

"You'll make it, won't you boys," he said, grabbing them.

"No!" Neera protested, but Kron had

already placed them high onto the rocks in full view of the Herd.

"Watch them!" he shouted to the Herd. "They're tough. And if they can do it, so can you!"

The Herd grumbled, but slowly started up the rocks. Kron smiled triumphantly.

"KRON!" a voice called out.

It was Aladar, and he was racing through the Herd as fast as he could. They all watched as he ran up to Kron.

"Kron, get the Herd out of here," he said, out of breath from running. "A carnotaur's coming." The Herd groaned.

"Keep moving," Kron said to the Herd.

"Stop!" Aladar protested. "I've been to the valley!" he continued. "There's a safer way."

"Kron, listen to him," Neera advised.

"Look," Aladar argued, "we've gotta go now!"

"Go where?" Kron snapped back. "Straight to the carnotaurs?"

"If we hurry, we can get around them," Aladar said. "We can't get over these rocks. There's a sheer drop on the other side."

Kron didn't want to listen. In frustration, he reached up and pushed the orphans a little higher.

"You're gonna kill the Herd!" Aladar shouted so everyone would hear. "I know a way to the valley and everybody can make it." He turned and addressed the Herd: "Now follow me!"

Kron had heard enough. He charged at Aladar.

"Kron!" Neera cried, trying to stop him, but he just shoved her out of the way. He landed squarely in front of Aladar, eyes ablaze.

"They're staying with me," he said menacingly.

Aladar ignored him. "All right," he said to the Herd. "Let's go."

Kron was enraged. He could not allow Aladar to challenge his authority anymore. He lunged, knocking Aladar into the rocks, but Aladar quickly recovered. He caught Kron by surprise with a lunge of his own, and Kron was knocked off his feet. Kron had the advantage of size, but Aladar was faster.

Kron was suddenly knocked to the ground.

It was Neera! She had belted him hard, knocking him right off his feet.

Neera helped Aladar to his feet. Together they headed off, and to Kron's astonishment, the Herd followed.

"Neera!" Kron yelled, but it was too late. The Herd had made up its mind.

Aladar began to lead the Herd out of the canyon with confidence, until he heard a terrifying roar.

Just ahead, blocking their way, was the gigantic, savage carnotaur.

"He led it right to us," Kron yelled to the Herd. Now the Herd was confused, and they started to panic. Dinosaurs scattered in all directions.

"No! Don't move," Aladar pleaded, "If we scatter, he'll pick us off!"

The Herd stopped to listen to him. "Stand together!" he urged.

Kron snorted, convinced that Aladar and the Herd were doomed. He started to climb the rocks. Looking back, he could see that the Herd had stopped, not knowing what to do.

The carnotaur, however, knew exactly

what to do. He charged into the Herd, stomping forward with ground-shaking force.

To everyone's amazement, Aladar stepped directly into the carnotaur's path, bellowing as loudly as he could.

Even the carnotaur was surprised, and he pulled back suddenly.

Then Neera joined in, along with one of the others. Then another joined them. And another.

The carnotaur was confused. He was not used to having other dinosaurs stand up to him.

Then he spotted Kron, still making his way up the landslide. Before anyone could react, the carnotaur broke away, leaping onto the rocks.

Neera knew where he was headed, though, and she raced off in pursuit, followed by Aladar.

"Kron!" Neera called out to him.

Kron looked back to see the carnotaur climbing after him. He was almost to the top, but he knew he had to climb faster. The carnotaur was gaining on him.

At last he was at the top—but as he reached up to pull himself over, he saw that Aladar was right: there *was* no other side, just a sheer drop—and it was a long, long way down.

The carnotaur was level with him now, and there was nowhere to go. Kron would have to face the carnotaur. It was his fate.

Kron lunged, but the carnotaur was ready for him. He stepped aside and grabbed Kron by the neck, cutting into the flesh with his jagged teeth. Kron howled in pain.

By the time Aladar and Neera reached the ledge, the fight was well under way. Kron fought bravely, but no single iguanodon, even the mighty Kron, was any match for a carnotaur.

They arrived just in time to see the carnotaur hurl Kron into a wall of rock. He crashed down with a *THUD*, soundly defeated. Kron tried to get up, but he couldn't move.

The carnotaur rose up in triumph. He never saw Neera, who broadsided him with all her strength and knocked him down.

The carnotaur quickly recovered and

jumped back to his feet. He slashed at Neera angrily, sending her flying into the rocks. The impact knocked the wind out of her, and before she could get up, the carnotaur had moved in for the kill.

But Aladar was right behind him, and with a swish of his tail, he struck the carnotaur hard across the face. The carnotaur respond-ed, lashing his own tail, but Aladar lunged at the carnotaur, ramming him backward. The rocks at the edge of the cliff began to crack and the carnotaur tumbled over the edge.

Aladar painfully pulled himself to safety. Neera rushed over to him, and the two of them peered over the cliff at the lifeless carnotaur. Then they remembered Kron and raced to his side. His wounds were deep, and he wasn't moving. There was nothing they could do for him. Aladar tried to comfort Neera as she leaned down beside her brother and put her head close to his.

After a moment, Neera nodded, and the two of them made their way back to the rocks.

The bellowing started as soon as they were

visible from the ledge. The entire Herd had gathered to greet them, trumpeting their appreciation. And though they were weary, wounded, and hurting, they had won the day. The Herd would survive—and there was a lake full of water waiting for them at—the Nesting Grounds.

"WELCOME HOME!" Aladar announced triumphantly. Neera smiled at him proudly as he led the Herd down the sloping mountainside and into the lush valley.

Epilogue

Large, healthy dinosaur eggs lay in the nest, with watchful eyes surrounding them.

"Move over," Eema said, making her way through. "Bringin' in babies is what I do best." One of the eggs started to crack.

"Look," Plio called to Yar and Eema, "somebody wants to meet you!"

The shell broke away to reveal a baby dinosaur.

"Oh, happy day!" said Eema.

"Well done, little one," Baylene added.

"Come here you little rascal," Yar said, picking up the baby. "Let me get a good look at you."

After oohing and ahhing over the baby, the group turned their attention to Zini, who had found some new friends—five pretty female lemurs. And they were paying attention to him!

"Any of you ladies up for a game of monkey in the middle?" he asked.

In the valley, mother dinosaurs tended to their nests, giant birds soared gracefully overhead, and a group of young dinosaurs played in the lake. Everywhere, there was peace and beauty.

Soon, the rest of the Herd joined in Aladar's celebration. The entire valley echoed with dinosaur voices. They all had their individual sounds, but they rang together as one.

DINOSAUR
tOys fRom MaTte

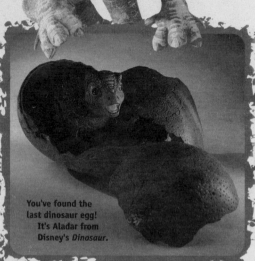

You've found the last dinosaur egg! It's Aladar from Disney's *Dinosaur*.

Dino Alive™! Aladar
You can hatch,"feed," and train your prehistoric pet again and again! Aladar will walk, talk, and ROAR just like in the movie!

Dinosaur Roaring Puzzle
The only Disney *Dinosaur* puzzle to come with sound! Hear Aladar "ROAR" when you piece together an actual scene from the movie!

Aladar Strikes Back! Giant Dinosau
Giant, dino-sized figure you make battle and roar.

Dino Clash Card Game
It's a prehistoric game of "War." Each player flips over a card...the most powerful card in each round wins!

Dinosaur Action Figures
All your favorite *Dinosaur* characters come to life with real roars, glowing eyes, and battle action! Collect all six!

Look for these and the other *Dinosaur* products:
Fossil Finder Activity Set & Adventures of Aladar Game